Halloween at the Haunted House

❧ A Glowing Mystery ❦

By Pamela Traynor

Illustrated by Maaz Farzaan

PAAT PRODUCTIONS

What kids and grown-ups are saying about the Glowing Mystery books:

"This book has all the elements of a page turner! Read the first part of the Glowing Mystery Series and you will be sure to get hooked!" —MagicBeans Bookstore

"This fast-paced chapter book is action-packed, funny and scary, but in the nicest possible way for young children. I can't wait to read the next book. —Reader's Favorite

"I read it to my second grade class and they didn't want me to put the book down." —Classroom Teacher

"The clues are perfectly placed and the plot is well-paced, picking up in intensity and raising goosebumps as one reads on." —Story Monster's Ink Magazine

"As an elementary school librarian, I am picky about the books I choose for my library. This book is a big hit." —Claudia

"I love love love your books." —Second Grader

TABLE OF CONTENTS

1: THE SCARIEST NIGHT 7
2: SECOND TOMB ROOM 16
3: SETTLING THE BET. 23
4: THE HAUNTED HOUSE 31
5: THE DISCOVERY. 38
6: BOARD MEETING OR BORED MEETING 46
7: THE OLD LIBRARY. 53
8: KNOCK, KNOCK 60
9: RETURN TO THE HAUNTED HOUSE . .67
10: BUMMED 75
11: HIDDEN PASSAGE 81
12: TREASURE. 88
13: MONEY MATTERS 95
14: BOOK RETURN. 100
15: THE BET 107
16: BONG!. 114

Sneak Peek! *Chaos at Camp Clover* 123
Kid's Page. 128
Resource Guide for Parents. 129
About the Author/Illustrator 130

Helping Your Child
Make the Transition to Chapter Books
A Free Resource Guide for Parents

See the back of the book for details
or visit PamelaTraynor.com

Text copyright © 2019 by Pamela Traynor
Illustration copyright © 2019 PAAT Productions

All rights reserved. Published by PAAT Productions

No part of this publication may be reproduced, stored in a retrieval system, or transmitted in any form or by any means, electronic, mechanical, photocopying, recording, or otherwise, without written permission of the publisher.

This book is a work of fiction. Names, characters, places, and incidents are either the product of the author's imagination or are used fictitiously, and any resemblance to actual persons, living or dead, business establishments, events, or locales is entirely coincidental.

ISBN 978-1-7343619-0-2 (paperback)

Printed in the U.S.A.
First Edition, December 2019
Illustrated by Maaz Farzaan
Edited by Qdmerit @ Fiverr.com

For those that built that spooky house
on the hill
so many years ago -

Thanks for the inspiration!

READ ALL THE Glowing Mystery Adventures

✤ THE SCARIEST NIGHT ✤
1 📖📖📖📖📖📖

The paper in Jason's hands shook as he walked to the front of the classroom. He had performed dozens of magic tricks at his school's talent shows, but this was different. He looked down at the words he had written—words that had come out of his head.

Would the class like it? Would his teacher be pleased? She taught her fourth graders how to write to entertain, and Jason learned that a good writer "hooks" the reader.

He looked at the kids sitting at their desks—waiting. He swallowed hard, took a deep breath and began . . .

The Scariest Night of My Life

by Jason Bean

We were standing in a hallway at the Haunted House. I was with two of my friends and my cousin, Beth. Every Halloween during Fright Fest, the Town of Mayville turns an old abandoned house into an attraction. The Haunted House is the best part of Fright Fest. This was my third time at the Haunted House, but this year was going to be different. Beth and my friends were trying to talk me out of it, but I wasn't budging. It was time for me

to take the Tomb Room Challenge!

The three Tomb Rooms are the scariest part of the Haunted House. Each one is dark and spooky. Cobwebs are everywhere and there's flickering candles on the walls. The first Tomb Room--Wimpy Warlocks--has one coffin in the center. You can go in this room with friends, but you can't come out until someone opens the coffin. The second Tomb Room is called Graduating Ghosts. It has five coffins, but you have to go in alone. I don't know what's in the third Tomb Room, Supreme Spooks, but no way was I ready for that. Even some of the older kids come out looking terrorized.

But I was ready for the second Tomb Room. I left the group and walked down the dark hallway. I grabbed the doorknob. My friends stood bug-eyed. There was no turning back. I twisted the handle and walked in. The room was dark. I took a few steps and the door slammed shut behind me. I jumped.

After my eyes got used to the dark, I could see picture frames on the walls. Ghoulish-looking faces stared out at me. They seemed to follow me with their eyes. My heart was pounding, but I forced myself to walk in.

Then I saw them—five coffins in a row covered with dust and cobwebs. Most kids can't even open one without wetting their pants.

The class giggled. Jason looked up and smiled. Then his eyes returned to his story.

If you open all five coffins, you get your picture up on the Halloween House Wall of Fame. That was my goal.

I started with the second coffin. A chill went down my spine as I got closer. I grabbed the lid. It wouldn't budge. I pulled harder. Suddenly the lid flew off and crashed to the floor.

I fell backward onto the first coffin. I peeked into the casket lined with red velvet cloth. But there was nothing--no body--no skeleton, only a card that said, 'Try another coffin—IF YOU DARE!'

I stepped around the lid and slowly walked to the fifth coffin. I knelt down. My hands were shaking as I placed my fingertips under the lid. I felt something on my hand and jumped back. It was a spider—a REAL one. I shook it off and grabbed the lid again. It opened easily with a long creeeeeak. I stared down at the inside of the coffin. I couldn't believe my eyes!

Jason looked up at the class and quietly spoke, "End of Part 1."

The class sat as if they were under a spell. Jason waited for his teacher to speak.

Finally, her voice broke the silence, "Well done, Jason. Very entertaining." The teacher walked over to Jason. "We look forward to hearing more next week."

As Jason walked back to his desk, kids were nodding and smiling. One boy reached out and gave Jason a high five. He had been to the Haunted House too.

But a few kids near the front still sat with their mouths open. They had *not* been to the Haunted House.

Jason took his seat. The girl in front of him turned and passed him a note. "It's from Owen," she whispered.

Owen sat in the front row.

Jason opened the small, crinkled piece of paper.

can you tell me and stanly about the hawnted house? we want to go this year

Jason wrote back:

come over tonight

meet me in my treehouse

Jason smiled and added a PS

PS If you dare!!!!!!!!

SECOND TOMB ROOM

📖 2 📖📖📖📖📖📖

"Wow, this is awesome!" Stanley said. "You're so lucky to have a treehouse."

"Yeah," Owen added. "This is way better than Peyton Parker's."

Stanley stuck his head out the window. "Are you kidding? You can hardly fit two people in Peyton's treehouse."

Jason grinned and patted himself on the chest. "And *I* helped build it."

Owen pointed to a wooden bench built into a wall of the treehouse. "What's that?"

"That's where I keep magic tricks and stuff. Wanna see my new trick?"

Stanley pulled his head back inside. "Yeah, *I* want to see it."

Jason started rummaging through the bench. "Shoot! I can't find it."

"Can't find what?" Stanley asked.

Jason smiled and brushed his hand against Stanley's ear. "Oh, here it is!" Then he extended his open palm. "My lucky coin!"

Stanley and Owen stared at the coin.

"Cool!" Stanley said.

"Yeah," Owen agreed. "Tell us about the Haunted House now."

"Okay." Jason tossed the coin in his bench and took out a flashlight.

The boys sat cross-legged facing Jason. He clicked on his flashlight and held it below his chin. His eyes got big as he leaned closer to his friends.

Suddenly a screen door slammed making the boys jump.

"Jason, five more minutes. It's getting dark." It was Mrs. Bean, Jason's mom.

"Okay, Mom," Jason called back.

"Come on," Owen urged. "Tell us about the Tomb Room."

"Yeah," Stanley said. He could hardly sit still. "My dad might take me this year."

Jason started speaking in a low, growly voice. "What I saw in the fifth coffin was . . ." He paused for dramatic effect. "a skeleton!"

The boys fell back as Jason jumped at them.

Owen shoved Jason. "No way!"

Jason nodded and continued. "And I think it was real too. And I knew I had to touch it to get

my name on the Haunted House Wall of Fame."

"Did you get your name on the wall?" Stanley interrupted.

"Let him finish," Owen said.

"I was about to touch it, but I saw a piece of paper in the skeleton's hand. I reached out to take it, and I thought the skeleton might grab me, so I did it quick."

Stanley leaned forward with his hands clasped. "What was the paper? What did it say?"

"It was too dark. I couldn't read it." Jason continued. "So I walked over to the flickering candle on the wall. I opened it and . . ." Jason stopped again to build suspense.

Owen whacked him on the knee. "Come on!"

Jason pretended he was holding the paper. "Go no further. Get out while you can. Do not open the first coffin."

"No way," Stanley said.

Owen stared at Jason. "What did you do?"

"I walked over to the first coffin in the row and was about to lift the lid, but I heard something."

"Wait!" Stanley held up his hand. "I *do* hear something."

Owen elbowed his friend. "You do not. It's your imagination. Let him finish."

Jason scrunched his fingers in the air. "It was a scratching sound coming from inside the coffin."

Owen grabbed Stanley. "Wait, I hear something too!"

Stanley stretched his neck up to look over Jason's spiky, brown hair. He stared wide-eyed pointing at the door.

Jason turned to see a huge, dark shadow in

the doorway of the treehouse. The three boys screamed at the same time. "*Ahhhhhhhh!*"

⇠SETTLING THE BET⇢

3

"What's going on?" Jason's cousin, Beth, stood at the top of the treehouse ladder. A big, puffy sleeping bag was strapped across her back, creating an extra-large shadow.

Owen held his chest. "Oh, Beth! It's you!"

"I *knew* I heard something!" Stanley remarked.

Jason grabbed Beth's outstretched hand and pulled her up. "What are you doing? What *is* all this stuff?"

Beth threw down her sleeping bag and backpack. "Mom said it's supposed to be a warm night, so I thought I'd settle our bet."

"What was your bet?" Owen asked.

Jason gestured toward Beth with his thumb. "This tumbleweed didn't think Ace McAllister survived the explosion in Monsters from Mars."

"They're not gonna kill off the head of the Monster Defense Agency." Owen shook his head.

"That's what *I* said." Jason smiled at Beth.

Jason and Beth were not only cousins, they were best friends *and* neighbors. They were always making bets with one another. Since Jason won the bet about Ace McAllister, it meant Beth had to sleep in the treehouse all alone.

Beth unzipped her backpack. "So what are you guys doing?"

"Jason is telling us about the Haunted House. I might go this year," Stanley said.

Beth stared at Stanley, and then turned to

Jason. "You didn't hear? They may not have the Haunted House this year."

"What!" Owen jumped up. "Why?"

"My mom said the roof may be leaking. They're not sure if it's in good enough condition. She's on the Mayville Town Board."

Stanley plopped on the floor with a dazed look. "No Haunted House," he murmured. "It's the best part of Fright Fest."

"And it raises a lot of money for our town too," Jason said.

"It's not definite," Beth said. "My mom is going over in the morning. She has to take pictures of any leaks to show the board. I'm going with her."

Jason's eyes lit up. "Can I go with you?"

"I'll ask." Beth unrolled her sleeping bag and

sat down. She pulled her tablet and a bag of chips from her backpack. "Well guys, I'm going to bed early tonight, if you don't mind."

Jason tossed his flashlight into his treehouse bench.

"Who's the dude," Owen nodded toward a sketch tacked on the wall.

Beth shot Jason a look.

He returned her stare and shook his head.

Beth and Jason had a secret. The old library in their school was haunted by a ghost named Hector McGreevy. The school librarian had been fired from the library long ago, but his ghost had returned to cause trouble.

It all started when Jason saw a glow on a shelf in the old library. He and Beth discovered that Hector was using a missing book to cause problems in their town. But when Jason and Beth found the book and got it back on the shelf, the glow disappeared, and that put an end to Hector's shenanigans. Afterward, Jason put up the sketch to remind him of their victory.

"Uh-uh, that's our great, great uncle," Beth piped up.

Owen raised an eyebrow as he looked from Beth to Jason. "Why do you have . . .?"

"Yoo-hoo!" Jason's mom called from the back door.

"I better get inside before my mom has a cow." Jason was happy for the interruption. He headed toward the treehouse ladder.

"But what about the story? What was the scratching sound? You didn't finish," Stanley moaned.

Owen followed Jason down the ladder. "We'll just have to wait to hear Part 2."

Beth poked her nose out the door. "G'nite, guys."

"I'll signal you later," Jason yelled back to his cousin.

Jason and Beth had invented their own form of Morse code. They made up flashlight signals that meant different things.

Beth slid into her sleeping bag and propped herself up on her pillow. "Now for Zombie Invaders." She poked around on her tablet until she found the game.

"What?" Beth's eyes darted to the ceiling of the treehouse. A glimmer of light flashed back and forth. "Jason."

She grabbed her flashlight and looked out to

see Jason's silhouette in his bedroom window. She counted three long flashes followed by one short flash.

"Transmission received," Beth said as she flashed the same message back to her cousin—"Goodnight."

～THE HAUNTED HOUSE～

"I hope we can have the Haunted House this year," Jason said.

He was sitting in the back seat of his aunt's car. Beth's mom was driving them to the Millington Mansion, otherwise known as the Haunted House. Beth sat in the front. It was a cool autumn day.

"Look," said Beth as they drove down Main Street. "They're hanging the Fright Fest banner. I can't believe Halloween is only a week away."

Jason pointed to a man on a ladder. "And they're getting the clock tower ready. I can't wait to hear it *bong*!"

The town square was in the center of the small community of Mayville. People were sitting on benches, walking dogs and pitching coins into the fountain. On one side of the town square stood the town hall and next to that was the hundred-year-old clock tower.

Every year, the week before Halloween, the clock tower would ring twice a day—twelve times at noon and twelve times at midnight. It helped usher in Fright Festival. Everyone in the town of Mayville loved this tradition.

Aunt Vicky glanced at Jason in the rearview mirror. "Well, Jason, we're a week from Halloween, so you just may hear the clock ring today."

Beth's mom passed through the town and

turned right. Then she continued driving down a road lined with trees.

"The leaves are getting colorful," Beth said. Then she turned to her mother. "Did anyone ever live in the Haunted House?"

Her mom answered. "Before it was the Haunted House, it was the Millington Mansion. Mr. and Mrs. Millington lived there for many years before Mrs. Millington died. Then Mr. Millington became a recluse and no one saw him anymore."

"What's a recluse?" Jason asked.

"A person who keeps to himself and doesn't care to be around people," his aunt answered.

"That's sad," Beth murmured.

Beth's mom continued, "The talk around town was that Mr. Millington became a bit paranoid.

The Millingtons were very wealthy. Neighbors said he began hiding his money because he was afraid someone would break in." She slowed the car and turned right.

A woman setting out pumpkins on her front porch, turned and waved as they drove by.

"So what happened?" Jason asked.

"After Mr. Millington died, they discovered he had no heir, so the town took possession of the house," Beth's mom said.

Jason looked confused. "What? Wait. Why did it matter that he had no hair?"

Beth rolled her eyes. "Not hair, heir. He had no family to leave the house to."

The car turned up a long, winding driveway.

At the top of a hill stood the Millington Mansion. Tall, pointy rooftops loomed into the

sky. Gray paint flaked off the walls of the house. The light coming through the front windows gave the appearance of two glowing eyes peering down at them as they approached.

"Whoa!" Jason said. "It still gives me the willies to see it."

Beth's mom parked the car and they walked up a path to the house. It was overgrown with prickly shrubs and bushes.

Beth stopped short and pointed to the weed-covered lawn. "What is *that*?"

"It's Mr. and Mrs. Millington," her mother explained. "Well, their *graves*. It was Mr. Millington's request that they be buried here."

"Ick," Beth said as she quickly tip-toed past.

Beth's mom led the kids around to the back.

"Do you have a key?" Jason asked.

"No need," Aunt Vicky said. "The lock on the back door is broken."

The door creaked open and they entered a dingy, gray kitchen.

"I'll only be a few minutes taking pictures upstairs, so don't wander off."

Jason rubbed his hands together. "Can we go down to the Tomb Rooms?"

"Absolutely not," said Aunt Vicky. "You can wait here on the first floor. Nowhere else." She gave her nephew a serious stare before pulling her phone from her purse. Then she disappeared up the back staircase.

"What do you want to do?" Beth asked.

Jason smiled at his cousin. "Let's explore!"

⇜THE DISCOVERY⇝
📖📖📖📖 **5** 📖📖📖📖

On the first floor of the Millington Mansion was a kitchen connected to a large dining room. Across the hall was a parlor and a study. The house was empty except for a few pieces of furniture covered with sheets.

"Nothing much to look at," Jason muttered walking from the parlor into the hallway. "It's more fun when it's all set up for Fright Fest."

"Come in here," Beth called.

Jason followed her voice into the study. On each wall were fancy bookcases that stretched from floor to ceiling. In the center of the room sat a massive wooden desk. The drawers had been removed.

Beth stared up at the bookcases that towered over their heads. "I wonder why they left all these books."

"Who'd want a bunch of dusty old books," Jason said pinching his nose. "They stink too!"

Jason spied a tall ladder. It was attached to a rail that ran across the top of the bookcase. "Look, this is how they reached the higher shelves." He grabbed a rung and started to climb.

"Be careful." Beth rushed over to hold the ladder as her cousin scrambled to the top.

Jason looked across the long shelves of books. "Push me to the end."

Beth leaned against the ladder making it creak slowly along the track. "See anything interesting?"

Jason's eyes darted from book to book. "Nah, looks like a lot of biographies." Then something caught his eye. "Wait—push me down further. I see one that has gold lettering on the spine."

"It's stuck," Beth said pushing on the ladder. "It won't move."

Jason held the ladder with one hand and leaned out with the other. His fingers were brushing the edge of the book. Using his pointer finger, he slowly nudged it out of its spot. "Get ready."

Beth held out her hands just as the dusty book dropped. "Oomph," Beth said catching it.

It was as thick as a dictionary with golden edging on the pages.

Beth blew away dust from the top, and then ran her fingers over the golden raised lettering

on the cover. "Secrets of Millington Mansion," she read.

Jason hopped off the ladder and peeked at the book's cover. "That's interesting."

Beth touched a black smudge near the bottom of the book. "It looks like somebody crossed words out."

Jason tilted the book toward his cousin. "Look! They did it on the spine too. Open it up."

Beth turned a couple pages until she reached the table of contents. She began to read the titles:

1. Construction of Millington Mansion
2. Tunnels and Trap Doors
3. Hidden Treasure

"Hey," Jason interrupted pointing to Chapter 3. "Your mom said Mr. Millington may have hidden money somewhere."

"No money was every found," Beth said leafing through the pages."

Jason laughed. "What—looking for money in the book?"

Then Jason jumped as Aunt Vicky walked into the study.

Beth placed her hand on her chest. "Jeez, Mom. You scared us!"

"Sorry kids." She frowned. "It doesn't look like we'll be able to open the Haunted House this year." She held up her phone. "I found some pretty bad water damage upstairs."

Jason moaned as if he were in pain. "Noooo."

Beth's mom slipped her phone into her purse. "We'll just have to see what the board says."

"Look what we found, Mom." Beth held up the book. "It's all about the Millingtons and this house. Can we borrow it?"

Beth's mom walked over to look at the book's cover. "Interesting," she said. "But, no Beth. This isn't a library and we can't be taking things from the house."

"We got it from up there," Jason said pointing to the top shelf where the ladder rested.

"That's okay. Just leave it on the desk." She turned to walk out. "I'm meeting with the town board in half an hour. We have to go."

Beth set the book on the desk and hurried after her mother.

Her mom walked to the front door and swung it open. "Oh!" she gasped.

On the other side of the door stood a short, balding man with his hands on his hips.

"No more Haunted House!" he snapped at the

three of them.

Jason, Beth and her mom stood dumbfounded as the little man ranted on.

He shook his fist in the air. "This place has *got* to go!"

BOARD MEETING OR BORED MEETING

Thirty minutes later, Jason and Beth were sitting in the back of the town hall board room. They promised Beth's mom they would be quiet during her meeting.

The man who confronted them at the Haunted House was Mr. Snarly. He was known around town as Sniveling Snarly because he was always complaining about something. His latest rant was about the Haunted House. As a neighbor of the Millington Mansion, he thought it was time the place be torn down.

"Now I know why they call these board

meetings," Jason whispered to Beth. "This is *boring!*"

"Shhh," Beth hushed her cousin. "They're starting."

Six people sat at a long table in the front of the room. Beth's mother was on the end. A large man wearing a brown suit rapped a gavel on the table. "The Mayville Town Council will begin its meeting. We'd like to welcome all Mayville Town citizens."

The man with the gavel scanned the crowd in front of him. He rolled his eyes when he saw Mr. Snarly sitting in the front row. Then he continued. "Today we will address the present state of the Millington Mansion and its future."

A half dozen hands shot in the air.

The town board president knew that it

was best to let Mr. Snarly have his say first. Otherwise, he'd be interrupting throughout the entire meeting. The man rapped his gavel again to quiet the crowd. "Order please." He took a deep breath before looking at Mr. Snarly. "Mr. Snivel—, uh—I mean, Mr. Snarly. Would you like to speak?"

Mr. Snarly stood up. "I'll be short."

Jason leaned over and whispered in Beth's ear. "He has to be short. He's five-two."

Beth covered her mouth to keep from giggling out loud.

Mr. Snarly walked back and forth as he spoke. "The Millington Mansion is a menace to the community and needs to be torn down. It's old and dilapidated. The roof is leaking and neighbors are complaining that they hear noises

at night and see things in the windows."

"Hmph," Jason breathed. "He's just making stuff up."

A man with a long beard leaned forward and spoke into his microphone. "Umm—Mr. Snarly, are you trying to tell us the Millington Mansion is haunted?"

"That's not for me to say," Mr. Snarly barked.

Beth's mom spoke next. "Are other neighbors complaining too, or is this just *your* concern, Mr. Snarly?"

Mr. Snarly's face turned red as he shook his fist in the air. "You'll see! I'll get names! I'm going to start a petition, then . . . then . . ." he stammered. "You'll see!"

Beth elbowed Jason in the ribs. Her eyes grew wide as she mouthed the words, "you'll see" to her cousin.

Mr. Snarly started walking down the aisle. "I'll be back," he threatened. Then he stopped and turned around. "And another thing—I hear the clock tower is broken. They can't get it to ring." He pointed a finger in the air. "That's a sign that the Haunted House must come to an end."

The group sat in silence as Mr. Snarly stormed out and slammed the door.

The town board members seemed to let out a collective sigh.

"Alright," said the man with the gavel. "Are there others who'd like to speak?"

Beth poked Jason again and pointed to the door. The two cousins slid out of their chairs and quietly walked out to the lobby.

"Did you hear what I heard?" Beth asked.

"Yeah," Jason answered. "Mr. Snarly said 'you'll see.' That's what Hector McGreevy was saying when people saw his ghost in the old library."

"Are you thinking what I'm thinking?" Beth asked.

Jason answered with another question. "That maybe somebody's behind this Millington Mansion mess?"

Beth slowly nodded her head.

Jason nodded too.

"Hector McGreevy," they said at the same time.

~THE OLD LIBRARY~

📖📖📖📖📖📖 7 📖

Beth crinkled her nose. "No wonder we needed a new library. It stinks down here."

"Yup, 14." Jason stopped. He'd been counting the steps. "Been down here so many times, I think I could walk these stairs blindfolded."

When their school built a new library and media center, Jason volunteered to help Miss Finn, the librarian. He had taken many trips down to the old library to help move all the books upstairs.

Beth peeked into the blackness. "I don't know why we have to come down here. The leaky roof,

Mr. Snarly's petition, the broken clock tower . . . we know Hector's ghost is behind all this."

Jason shined his light down the center aisle and hesitated before taking another step.

"Before we go searching all over for a missing book, we have to know for sure. Finding the glow will be the proof we need."

"Okay," Beth said giving her cousin a little push.

The flashlight beam swayed back and forth as they walked.

"You know, we have to make a bet. We haven't made one in a while," Beth said leaning close to her cousin.

"Yeah, but not *now*. And can you give me some room? I can feel your breath on my neck."

After a few more steps, Beth grabbed her

cousin's arm. "Look." She pointed to the left.

With the flashlight off, they noticed a small glow halfway down the aisle. The tiny light it cast made it look like a lightning bug resting on the shelf.

Jason quickly walked toward the glowing space.

Beth was tight on his heels. "Isn't this the same aisle as the book about the Mayville Town Fair?"

"Yeah, aisle 9," Jason whispered. He shone the beam of light across the book spines. "Local history. That makes sense if it's a book about the Millingtons."

"But we still need to get the call number, right?" Beth asked. "So you can look it up on the school computer?"

Jason looked surprised. "I'm impressed you remembered that."

Beth stared up at the glowing space. "How are we supposed to reach that shelf? There's no ladder here like in the Millington house."

Jason crouched and patted his shoulders. "Come on, I'll give you a lift."

Beth laughed. "Are you crazy?"

"You may be a year older than me, but I'm bigger." Jason said.

"Okay," Beth said swinging her legs over Jason's shoulders. "It's *your* back."

"Uumph." Jason took a deep breath as he stood up and grabbed the bookcase to steady himself. "Can you see the numbers?"

"Move to the right a little," Beth said.

"Okay, stop." Beth leaned on the shelf and

craned her neck upward.

Jason started to squirm. "What's taking so long?" he complained.

"Give me a sec. I'm trying to memorize the numbers next to the glow. Be quiet."

Jason rolled his eyes as he swayed back and forth.

"Okay, got it. Put me down."

Jason knelt and Beth slipped off his shoulders. Then he reached into his back pocket and pulled out a pencil and little notepad. "Here." He handed them to his cousin.

Beth raised her eyebrows. "Wow—'Mr. Prepared'. You should be a Boy Scout."

Beth jotted down the numbers and handed the notebook back. "Do your thing, Beanarino."

Jason slid the notebook back into his pocket.

"This is perfect timing. I'm helping Miss Finn in the library this afternoon. I can search for the title then. Let's go."

"The glow seems so tiny compared to the last time we were down here," Beth said. "Remember how bright it was?"

Jason nodded. "That's because it took us so long to track down that zombie book. Hector was at peak power *then*. He's just getting started now."

Jason and Beth took the steps two at a time. When they reached the top, Jason grabbed the doorknob.

"Uh-oh," Jason whispered. "We're locked in."

⇜ KNOCK, KNOCK ⇝
📖 📖 📖 📖 📖 📖 📖 **8**

"What are we going to do?" Beth whispered.

"I don't know," Jason whispered back.

Beth nudged Jason with her elbow. "Try knocking."

"I'm really not supposed to be down here unless I have a reason," Jason muttered.

"We have a reason." Beth pushed past her cousin and began knocking on the door. "This is like when I was trapped in the bathroom at the movie theater. Hello?" She pounded harder.

"Shhh, listen." Jason held up his hand.

They stood as still as statues as the sound of

heavy footsteps approached on the other side. The knob began to jiggle. Then the door swung open.

"Mr. Winston!" Jason and Beth exclaimed together. It was their school custodian. He had warned them about Hector McGreevy.

He looked at the kids sternly. "What are you up to?" He held up his hand. "Never mind—I don't want to know."

Jason and Beth stepped out into the hall.

"Thanks, Mr. Winston," said Jason. He was eager to go, but he knew the custodian had more to say.

The old man continued. "I told you nothing good will come out of going down there. You ought to be glad I had to mop this hallway or you might've been stuck in there all day."

"We know, we're sorry," Beth said.

Mr. Winston stood shaking his head as Jason and Beth took off down the hall.

"Knock, knock," Beth whispered in her cousin's ear.

Jason was sitting at a computer in the back of the new library. He smiled, but didn't take his eyes off the screen. "Who's there?"

"Phillip."

"Phillip who?" Jason asked.

"Phillip my bag with candy, please!"

Beth forced a laugh. "Isn't that a good one?" She pulled out a chair and sat beside her cousin. "I got an idea for our next bet."

Jason finally turned to his cousin and raised an eyebrow. "I'm intrigued. Go on."

Beth's eyes lit up. "Whoever gets the most Halloween candy wins the bet. The loser has to carry the winner's backpack to school for a month."

Jason frowned. "That won't work. We always go together. We'll have the same amount."

"Maybe not. Sometimes people toss in more than one piece when you're lucky," Beth said. "Come on. It'll be fun. When we get back to my house, we can count it."

"Okay," Jason said turning back to the screen.

Beth opened a folder, pulled out a sheet of paper and started reading to her cousin. "Did you know that the first jack-o-lanterns were made of gourds, not pumpkins?"

Jason looked annoyed. "What are you doing here?"

"My class is doing pumpkin research," Beth said. "Did you find out the name of the missing book?"

Jason shifted in his chair and gave his cousin a stern look. "I'm trying to right now, but I keep getting interrupted."

Beth held her fingers to her lips and turned an invisible key.

Jason's hands returned to the keyboard. After a few clicks, he stopped and pointed at the screen. "Here it is."

Beth leaned over and read the title aloud, "'Secrets of Millington Mansion.' Hey, that's the book we found at the Haunted House. I thought it belonged to Mr. Millington."

"Yeah, me too," Jason said. "But remember how some of the words were blackened out on the cover? I bet he borrowed it and decided to keep it for himself."

Beth shrugged. "This is gonna be easy peasy. We know *right* where the book is." She grabbed her cousin's arm. "Hey, let's get it right after school."

Jason shook his head. "I don't know. Your mom said it doesn't belong to us."

Beth piped up. "Well, it doesn't belong to Mr. Millington either."

Jason thought for a moment. "Alright. I guess." Jason gave in.

"Let's meet at the bike rack after school." Beth jumped up and pushed in her chair. "I gotta go."

She started to walk away, but stopped and whispered to her cousin. "Don't wimp out on me. We gotta get the book back before Hector becomes more powerful."

♠ RETURN TO THE HAUNTED HOUSE ♠
9 📖📖📖📖📖📖

Jason and Beth were on their way back to the Haunted House. As they approached, Jason slowed his bike and held out his arm to signal Beth to stop. He pointed to a small figure in the distance. Mr. Snarly stood holding a clipboard as someone signed his petition.

Beth drew in a breath. "Wow—he's really getting signatures."

"Let's leave our bikes here in the bushes," Jason said. "I don't want to take a chance of running into him."

"Good idea," Beth said walking her bike off

the sidewalk.

Jason went first and pushed his way through the tall, overgrown bushes that surrounded the Millington property. Branches and brambles caught on their clothes as they made their way to the back door.

"Hope there's no poison ivy in here," Beth said pushing a branch from her face.

Jason opened the back door, and they walked through the kitchen into the hallway. "Let's be quick before Mr. Snarly comes snooping around."

"I wonder why Hector's making it so easy to find the book," said Beth. "Usually we have to search and search."

Jason walked to a front window in the parlor and peeked from behind the curtain. "Snarly's still out there."

Beth walked into the study. "Oh no," she yelled. "I was wrong. Hector's *not* making it easy."

Jason ran into the room and looked at the desk. The book was gone!

Jason hurried over and dropped to his knees. He desperately felt around the empty slots of the desk. "That's impossible. I left it right here." He looked up at Beth. "You saw me."

"I did. But this is how Hector McGreevy works!" A wave of panic washed over Beth's face. "Oh my gosh. I bet we won't be able to get out." She rushed to the kitchen.

"What in the world?" Beth called.

Jason ran to the kitchen. "Are we locked . . . what?" He looked up.

They stood staring. The cabinets and cupboards in the kitchen were wide open.

"We just walked through here. Who did this?" Beth asked.

"It's Hector. He's distracting us. Come on. Help me look for the book."

They raced back to the study.

Jason pointed to the bookcase. "Look! The ladder was moved. Maybe the book is back on the shelf. You check this side. I'll check over there."

Beth started scanning the bottom row. She pointed as she searched each row for the book with golden letters.

Suddenly, Jason and Beth stopped and looked up as heavy footsteps pounded above their heads.

Beth turned to Jason with wide eyes.

The footsteps got louder. It sounded like a five-hundred-pound gorilla was upstairs.

"J-J-Jason," Beth stammered. "We *have* to get out of here."

"But we've got to find the *book*," Jason pleaded.

"If we don't leave now, we might be trapped in here," Beth said. "Come on!"

Jason gave in and followed his cousin. They burst through the kitchen door and sprinted for the path.

Beth started to push through the woody trail.

Jason called. "What are we gonna do?"

Beth turned back to answer her cousin. "I don't know, but . . . Ahhhhh!" Beth froze as something grabbed her wrist. She shook her arm frantically.

Jason ran up behind her.

"Ah-hah!" A short, balding man burst through the bushes, just as Beth jerked her arm free.

"Mr. Snarly?" she gasped.

The little man's face was redder than a beet. "I heard all that noise! I *told* you that place is haunted!"

Jason walked on ahead ignoring the ranting little man. "Come on, Beth."

Mr. Snarly tried to follow, but his pants caught on a bramble bush. "You shouldn't be hanging around here. I'm gonna tell your mother." His voice faded as they reached their bikes, but he continued to yell. "I've got fifteen names on my list."

Beth pulled her bike from the bushes. "See, he really thinks that place is haunted."

"But we know it's not," Jason said. "It's just

Hector causing trouble again."

Jason and Beth hopped on their bikes.

"It'll be horrible if there's no more haunted house," Jason said. "We've got to save it."

~BUMMED~

"So what are you gonna be for Halloween?" Beth asked Jason.

They were in his treehouse. Beth was stretched out on the floor drawing scary faces in a sketchbook. Jason sat with his hand out trying to roll a quarter across the back of his knuckles.

"'Monster from Mars.' Remember?" Jason said with a tone. "I told you I already have the mask."

Jason and Beth were obsessed with monsters and zombies.

"Okay, well you don't have to bite my head

off," Beth remarked.

"Sorry," Jason said picking up the coin that had rolled across the floor. "I'm just so bummed there won't be a Haunted House this year—maybe never again! I really wanted to do the third Tomb Room."

Beth looked up surprised. "You mean . . . Supreme Spooks?"

"Yeah, but now it'll never happen."

"I'm gonna be a zombie," Beth said trying to change the subject.

"You were a zombie last year," Jason said.

"I know, but it's easy. I still have the old, ripped clothes and the makeup. Besides some people gave me extra candy because they liked my costume so much," Beth said grinning.

Jason nodded at his cousin. "Oh—the bet!"

He opened the lid of his wooden bench, tossed in the coin and took out a little notepad and pencil. Flipping to a blank page, he looked at his cousin. "Okay, what's our plan?"

Beth paused her marker. "What plan?"

"To get the book. It has to be in the Millington House somewhere! We've got to find it!"

"I don't know, Jason. We might need to give this one up. My parents won't be too happy if their only daughter gets trapped in a haunted house, never to return."

Jason got jumpy with excitement. "But I have an idea. What if . . ."

"Beth," a voice was calling in the yard. "Are you up there?" It was Beth's mom.

"Yes." She peeked out of the treehouse door and looked down at her mother.

"I need you to run an errand for me." Mrs. Goodwin stood with her hand up blocking the sun from her eyes.

"Right now?" Beth groaned.

"I need you to go over to the Millington House and get some papers."

Jason jumped up and looked at Beth, then back at his aunt. "Okay, we can go!"

"What are the papers?" Beth asked climbing down.

"There's some men over there looking at the roof. They're going to give us an estimate of how much it'll cost to fix it."

Jason's eyes lit up. "Really?"

"What about Mr. Snarly's petition?" Beth asked.

Mrs. Goodwin shrugged. "I don't have any

control over what that man does. I just do my job. The board wants to see if it's something we can afford to fix."

Beth smirked at her cousin. "I guess you get your wish."

"I'm gonna get my bike," Jason yelled running to the house.

"The men will give you an estimate of how much it costs to fix the roof. That's what you need to bring back to me," said Beth's mom.

"Got it," Beth said."

HIDDEN PASSAGE
11

"There's the roof people," Beth said hopping off her bike.

Two men were on the porch of the Millington Mansion. A tall, thin man was sitting on the top step eating a sandwich. A heavy-set man wearing a tool belt was talking on a cell phone.

As Jason and Beth walked up to the porch, the man with the sandwich looked up. He wiped his mouth with the back of his hand. "Hey, there."

"Hi. I'm Beth Goodwin. This is Jason. My mom sent us to get the papers about the roof."

"Do you think you can fix it?" Jason asked.

"Don't know yet," said the thin man. "Gonna go look now."

The man on the phone hung up and smiled at the kids. "Who do we have here?"

The thin man popped the last bit of sandwich in his mouth and mumbled, "We gotta give the estimate to these kids when we're done."

"Okay," said the heavy-set man as he reached for the front door.

"Can't get in that way," Jason said. "Follow us."

As they walked into the kitchen, the heavy-set man glanced down at his paperwork. "Says the leak's on the third floor."

"You know," the thin man spoke. "Some people are saying this place is haunted. Maybe we oughta call those ghost-bust people first." He let out a big laugh.

"Yeah, right." The heavy-set man started up the back staircase. "We won't be long," he shouted.

Beth raised her eyebrows. "Hope they don't run into you-know-who."

With the men out of sight, Jason whispered excitedly. "Okay, I think you should look through the kitchen cabinets. Maybe they were open the other day for a reason. I'll start looking in the parlor and dining room. And then we'll look in the study again.

Beth saluted her cousin. "Okay, boss."

Jason disappeared into the hall as Beth started opening each cabinet. "Nope, nope, nope," she chanted as she looked.

Jason walked into the dining room and stopped

beneath a huge, glittery chandelier. He turned in his spot. "Nowhere to hide a book in here." He sprinted to the parlor.

Jason began lifting the sheets that had been draped over the furniture.

Beth called. "Nothing in the kitchen. I'm heading to the study."

Jason met his cousin in the hall. "No luck in there either."

They walked into the study and stared up at the massive wall of books.

Beth walked closer to the shelves. "Okay, this is where I was looking before. Remember, it has gold lettering."

Jason walked to the middle of the bookcase. Using his finger like a laser, he started at the top and scanned back and forth on each shelf.

"I hope we find it before those men come back," Beth said keeping her eyes on the books.

When Jason was almost done searching, he approached the bookcase. "This ladder is blocking some of the books." He gave it a tug. With a squeak, the ladder rolled from the corner. Jason knelt down to look at the last few shelves. "It's dark in this corner."

"Wait! Look!" Jason yelled.

Beth ran over to where Jason crouched. "Did you find it?"

"No, but this book has the same fancy gold lettering," Jason said.

"What's it called?"

Jason tilted his head to read the spine. "'Hidden Passage.'"

Beth grabbed her cousin's arm. "Hey,

remember there was a chapter in the book called, 'Tunnels and Trap Doors?' Maybe this book will give us a clue."

Jason tried to pull the book from the shelf. "I can't get it. It's stuck."

"Pull harder," Beth said.

Jason used both hands. Suddenly, the top of the book tilted out and made a clicking sound.

Jason fell back onto the floor as a whole section of the bookcase swung inward revealing a dark, hidden passage.

TREASURE
12

"What in the world?" Beth stared into a dark tunnel.

Jason brushed dust from his pants. "Wow, there really *are* hidden tunnels in this place. I'm gonna check it out."

Beth grabbed his arm. "Do you think that's a good idea? What if those men come back?" Beth said looking toward the door.

Jason looked at his cousin like she had three heads. "Are you crazy? We haven't come this far to wimp out now."

"Oh, alright. But be careful and be quick."

Jason dropped to the floor and scooched himself into the dark hole. Like a soldier on the battlefield, he shimmied in until only his feet were visible.

"See anything?" Beth whispered.

"Just dark," Jason's voice echoed back. "Wish I had my flashlight." He used his elbows to crawl in a few more feet. "Yuck," he said swiping at a cobweb above his head.

"Anything?" Beth asked again.

Jason's hand reached out through the darkness and struck a wall. "No. Dead end," he murmured.

Jason was about to reverse directions. He leaned against the end of the tunnel. The wall moved and swung inward. "Wait," he shouted to Beth. "There's a door."

He reached through the opening to pull

himself forward and his hand struck something hard. He patted around a flat, metal box. "I found something!"

"We're all done."

Beth jumped, and then turned to see the two roof workers standing in the doorway.

"Where's your friend?" said the tall, thin man looking around.

"Uhh-uhh . . ." Beth stammered. "He'll be right back."

The man shrugged his shoulders. "Well, we've gotta write up the estimate. We'll meet you on the porch." The two men walked toward the kitchen.

Beth squatted and whispered loudly into the dark hole. "Jason, come on. Come back out."

Beth could see her cousin's feet inching

toward her. Then he stopped.

"Pull me out," he called.

Beth grabbed her cousin's feet and tugged. Jason slid out of the tunnel. His arms were wrapped around an old, metal box.

"What's that?" Beth asked.

"I don't know." Jason stood up and brushed cobwebs from his arms and legs.

Beth pointed to the kitchen. "Those men are done. They have to do some paperwork and they want us to meet them on the front porch."

Jason stared at the box as he carried it to the desk. "Not before we open this." He set it down and pressed a small latch on the side of the lid. The top sprang open revealing a book and a large brown envelope.

"That's it!" Beth read the title on the book.

"*Secrets of Millington Mansion.*"

"Yes," Jason cheered. "We got it!" He reached out and picked up the bulky brown envelope. "I wonder what this is?"

Jason opened the flap of the envelope. His eyes grew big as he tilted it to show his cousin.

"OMG!" Beth's eyes nearly popped out of their sockets. "Mr. Millington *did* hide money in the house." She stared at the wad of cash Jason pulled out.

"Kids?" A voice called from the front porch. "We're done."

Jason stuffed the money back in the envelope and pushed the package into the waistband of his pants. He untucked his shirt to cover the bulge.

"Here." Jason handed the book to Beth. "Slide this in the back of your pants."

As they walked through the kitchen, Jason stopped and turned to Beth. "Let's go get the papers."

~MONEY MATTERS~

📖📖📖📖 **13** 📖📖

"Did you hide it good?" Jason asked Beth as she walked out of the garage.

"Yes. It'll be safe until we can bring it back to the old library." Beth rubbed her hands together and smiled at Jason with a mischievous grin. "*That* will put a stop to Hector . . . *and* Mr. Snarly."

Jason reminded his cousin of their last adventure. "Remember when I hid the zombie book in my treehouse, and it started glowing? We don't want anyone to see it."

"Stop worrying." Beth reassured her cousin.

They walked into Beth's kitchen to find Mrs. Goodwin talking on the phone. She held up her hand.

Beth waved the papers in front of her mother.

Mrs. Goodwin ended the call and set her phone on the table. "I'm afraid that was bad news. Mr. Snarly has hired a demolition company." Mrs. Goodwin stood shaking her head. "That mean little man has convinced dozens of neighbors to sign his petition."

Jason shot his cousin a look as she handed the papers to her mom.

Mrs. Goodwin glanced down to the bottom of the estimate. She pulled out a chair and sat down. "My goodness. We can't afford this!" She tossed the papers onto the table.

Beth gave Jason a nudge. "Show my mom

what we found."

Mrs. Goodwin looked confused as she watched her nephew pull a large envelope from the waistband of his pants.

"Maybe you can use this. We found it hidden in the Haunted House, I mean the Millington Mansion," Jason said.

Beth took the envelope and dumped the cash on the table. "This could help pay for the roof."

Mrs. Goodwin sat wide-eyed. "So he *did* hide money in the house." She pushed the money around with her hand. "Well, it certainly is more than we need for the roof, but then there's Mr. Snarly." She shook her head.

Beth walked closer to her mother. "But Mom, you told us you have no control over Mr. Snarly— you can only do *your* job. You should bring this

money to the board and let *them* decide."

Mrs. Goodwin gave Beth a squeeze. "I have a smart daughter. You're right. That's what I'll do."

Mrs. Goodwin stuffed the money into the envelope and walked out of the kitchen.

Beth frowned at her cousin and spoke in a whisper. "More problems. Hector's powers are growing. We've got to put a stop to Hector . . . and Mr. Snarly."

Jason spoke in a serious tone. "We can't wait any longer. Let's get the book and go to the old library *now*."

BOOK RETURN
14

"Do you think a custodian will be there?" Beth asked.

Jason and Beth were riding their bikes to school. They slowed down as they approached an intersection.

Jason stopped and reached out to press the cross button. "There usually is."

"On no, maybe it's too late. Look!" Beth pointed up the street.

A large truck was heading their way, with *Dugan's Demolition* printed on the side. It was pulling a flatbed trailer that carried a wrecking ball."

Jason shouted as the truck roared by. "Mr. Snarly is moving fast. Come on, we've got to hurry!"

As they rode up to the bike rack, Jason pointed to a car in the parking lot. "I think that's Mrs. Jennings' car."

The custodian was cleaning the front door windows when Jason walked up and rapped on the glass. Mrs. Jennings smiled and held the door open. "Hey kids, what are you doing here on a Saturday?

"Is it okay if we dash to the library?" Jason asked. "We'll only be a second."

"Sure. But don't be long. I'm leaving as soon as I finish here."

"Thanks, Mrs. Jennings. We'll be quick,"

Beth called back. They sprinted down the hall and around the corner.

Jason paused before opening the door to the old library.

"Okay, get ready to sweat like last time," Beth said.

But when Jason opened the door, it wasn't a blast of heat that hit them in the face. It was a howling, cold burst of air.

"OMG!" Beth yelled. "Hector wants to *freeze* us out. And listen . . . there's that pounding sound again!"

A loud banging echoed up from the darkness below.

"We've got to get to the glow. Hector's powers are out of control!" Jason clicked on his flashlight and aimed it on the steps as they hurried down.

The tiny glow they saw a couple of days ago was as bright as a stadium light. They raced down the center aisle.

"Whoa!" Jason yelled as he skidded to a stop. Beth plowed into the back of him. "Oomph!"

It was snowing in Aisle 9! Large snowflakes fluttered down from the ceiling. Icicles hung from the shelves.

Beth hugged her arms in front of her. "I-I-I'm freezing."

"I know. Me too, but we've got to get the book back." Jason ran to the glow and started pulling books off the shelf.

"Wh-what are you doing?" Beth's teeth chattered as she tried to speak.

"We're gonna have to climb up. It'll take both of us to push it back in its spot. Remember how

it repelled us last time?"

They breathed on their hands to warm them, and then began climbing to the glowing space on the shelf. As they reached the spot, Jason pulled the book from the back of his pants and held it up to the glowing space.

"Ready?" he called.

Jason struggled to keep the book from falling to the floor. He leaned on the shelf and placed his palm over the spine. "Help me push," he screamed.

Beth clung to the bookcase with one hand and placed her free hand over Jason's. "1, 2, 3, push!"

For a second the book resisted, but then like a black hole in outer space, the book was sucked into its spot.

Jason and Beth slid down the bookcase and collapsed onto a mound of snow.

All at once, the flakes stopped falling and snow began melting around them. The banging slowed to a tap, and then stopped completely.

As the air warmed, Beth and Jason stood up.

"I can feel my fingers again," Beth said staring at her outstretched hands. She breathed a heavy sigh. "We did it again. We defeated Hector McGreevy."

Jason started jogging back to the center aisle. "I know, but now we have to stop Mr. Snarly and his wrecking ball—if it's not too late."

☙ THE BET ☙

📖 📖 📖 📖 📖 📖 **15**

"Look—your parents." Jason pointed down the street.

Mr. Snarly and a group of people stood on the sidewalk in front of his house. Beth's parents stood facing him. Her mom held papers in her hand.

Jason and Beth saw the wrecking ball in front of the Millington Mansion. They could hear Mr. Snarly grumbling on.

"I don't care if you have money to fix the roof. That's not the only issue. What about the shadows I see, er . . . I mean shadows *we* see in the windows? What about the noises in the night?"

"Really, Mr. Snarly?" Mrs. Goodwin piped up. "You're a grown man. Do you really think there are ghosts in Millington Mansion?"

Mr. Snarly stuck his nose in the air. "You can't prove that there aren't."

"Yes, we can!" Jason announced riding up on his bike.

The entire crowd turned and stared at Jason.

"Jason?" Mrs. Goodwin said surprised. "What are you talking about?"

"We're *certain* the Millington Mansion isn't haunted. Right, Beth?"

"Right." Beth nodded.

"We'll prove it," Jason continued. "We'll spend the night in the Millington Mansion."

A gasp went up through the crowd.

Mrs. Goodwin eyes popped. "Jason! I don't know about that."

"Great idea!" Mr. Goodwin stepped forward and put his hand on his daughter's shoulder. "We'll camp out tonight. Let's make a bet, Mr. Snarly. If we don't see any ghosts, will you be willing to call off the wrecking ball?"

The crowd was silent as they waited for Mr. Snarly's response. "I guess." He made a face. "But I'll be watching too! —and listening!"

Mr. Goodwin leaned down and whispered to Jason and Beth. "Better get your sleeping bags ready."

The threesome decided to camp out in the parlor. Their sleeping bags were laid side by side

in the middle of the room.

Jason watched his uncle tend to a small fire in the fireplace. The flames grew and brightened the room.

"Oooh, that feels good." Beth extended her palms toward the flames.

"Can we stay up 'til midnight to see if the clock tower rings?" Jason asked.

Mr. Goodwin laughed as he pulled something out of his bag. "Go for it. *If* you can stay awake." He sat down on his sleeping bag and held a flashlight below his chin. His eyes grew big as saucers and flickered in the light of the fire. In a sinister voice he began reading from a book. "It was a dark, dark . . ."

"Wait!" Beth reached over and pulled a bag of popcorn from her backpack.

Mr. Goodwin started again. "It was a . . ."

"What was that?" Jason grabbed Beth's arm.

They stared into the hall.

"I heard it too." Beth said.

Mr. Goodwin got up and walked toward the door. "You two stay here."

"Be careful, Dad," Beth said inching a little closer to her cousin.

The kids sat in silence as the fire crackled and hissed. A minute passed as they strained to listen for Mr. Goodwin's footsteps.

Beth was about to get up, when her father appeared in the doorway. He was laughing as he walked over to Jason and Beth and held out an open palm. In it were a few pieces of broken acorns. "It was a squirrel. Must have crawled through the hole in the roof. I shooed it out the kitchen door."

"I should have brought peanuts, too." Beth laughed popping a piece of popcorn in her mouth.

Mr. Goodwin yawned. "Well, I'm hitting the hay."

"What about the story?" Jason whined.

Mr. Goodwin tossed the book and flashlight to his nephew. "You two can read."

Beth crawled into her sleeping bag. "I'm tired too. This has been an exhausting day."

"Jeepers," Jason complained. "We're staying in a haunted house and you two want to *sleep*?"

"It's not haunted, Jason," Mr. Goodwin murmured into his pillow.

Jason crawled into his sleeping bag and closed his eyes. He listened hard—hoping to hear the chime of the clock tower.

BONG

16

It took a few minutes for Jason to remember where he was. He rubbed his eyes to see Beth still curled up in her sleeping bag. He stretched and rolled over. His uncle's empty sleeping bag lay in a clump.

Jason sat up and looked around. "Uncle Tim?" he whispered. He pulled his feet out of his bag and tiptoed into the hall. "Uncle Tim?"

Jason's heart started to beat faster as he walked from room to room. "Uncle Tim?" Jason shouted.

"In here," came a voice.

Jason walked to the study and found his uncle standing in front of the massive bookcases.

"Look at all these books!" Mr. Goodwin stood with his hands on his hips. "Bet there's a lot of history here."

Jason sighed. "You scared me. I didn't know where you were."

Jason's uncle tussled his nephew's hair. "No worries. There's no ghosts in *this* place." He grinned. "And I think it's time to go tell Mr. . . . ."

"What's going on?" Beth stood in the doorway rubbing her eyes. Strands of her hair stuck out in all directions.

"Mornin', sunshine," Mr. Goodwin said. "We've banished the ghosts."

"Yeah," Jason interrupted. "And we're gonna go tell Mr. Snarly now, right Uncle Tim?"

"Yup," Mr. Goodwin said. He gave his daughter a little squeeze as he walked past. "Let's go pack up."

Jason and Beth got changed and rolled up their sleeping bags while Mr. Goodwin cleaned the ashes from the fireplace. The three grabbed their bags and headed for the front door.

"I can't wait to see Mr. Snarly's face when we tell him this place isn't haunted," Jason said.

Mr. Goodwin swung open the front door.

"What in the world?" Beth exclaimed.

On the porch stood Mr. Snarly, several neighbors and two men with Dugan's Demolition printed on their shirts. There were more neighbors on the lawn and a group of kids standing at the gate. Directly in front of the door, stood Mrs. Goodwin with her hand still in the air. She was

about to knock.

Mr. Goodwin gave his wife a peck on the cheek. "G' mornin' sweetheart," he whispered walking around her. Mr. Goodwin stopped on the top step of the porch and looked out at the crowd. Everyone waited in silence. He raised his arms in the air. "No ghosts," he announced.

A cheer went up from the crowd. Everyone began whooping and high fiving. A kid from their school started chanting. "Ghost chasers! Ghost chasers!" The entire crowd joined in.

Mr. Goodwin walked over to Mr. Snarly. "Well, Mr. Snarly, the board is ready to fix the roof. What do you say? Are you going to keep your word?"

The little man stood with a sour look on his face. He began ranting again. "But what about the clock tower? It's still broken." He turned toward the crowd and pointed a finger in the air. "That's a sign. There's still . . ."

Mr. Snarly's lecture was cut short. At that very moment, everyone's eyes lit up as they listened—*Bong! Bong! Bong!*

The cheering began again. All eyes were on Mr. Snarly as he slowly reached into his shirt pocket and drew out a folded piece of paper. He stared at it for a moment, and then--looking at Mr. Goodwin--he held up the petition and tore it in two.

As the pieces fluttered to the ground, Jason thought he detected a slight smile on Mr. Snarly's face.

Without a word, the little man turned and walked down the porch. The crowd parted to let him pass.

As the group started to break up, a new cheer began. "Haunted House! Haunted House!"

The two men wearing Dugan's Demolition shirts shrugged and headed for their truck.

Beth smiled up at her father. "Thanks, Dad."

"Yeah, Uncle Tim," Jason said. "Thanks."

Mr. Goodwin headed down the porch steps. "You can return the favor by getting your pictures up on the Haunted House Wall of Fame."

They all laughed.

ᕯEPILOGUEᕯ

Beth beamed as she walked out of the second Tomb Room. "I did it," she said proudly.

Jason gave his cousin a pat on the back. "Congratulations, Graduating Ghost."

"So how was it?" she asked. "What's the *third* Tomb Room like?"

Beth waited for Jason to answer.

He reached up and gestured like he was turning a key to lock his lips.

"Oh, you stink." Beth gave him a push.

At the end of the hallway, they walked up a dimly lit staircase. Flickering candles lined the walls. At the top, they slowed down to look at dozens of pictures hanging on the Wall of Fame.

"Here we are," Beth called.

Jason looked up at two shiny new frames hanging in the top row.

"It's cool they put up *both* our faces." Beth chuckled.

"Well, we *did* save the Haunted House," Jason said.

"No thanks to Hector McGreevy," Beth added. "Hopefully, we've seen the end of him."

Jason and Beth continued down the hall and walked out the exit.

"Whoa!" Beth said surprised.

There was a long line of people waiting to get into the Haunted House.

"Wait a minute!" Jason pointed to a small figure at the end of the line. "Isn't that Mr. Snarly?"

Beth's mouth dropped open as she spotted the little man. Then she held her hands to her mouth and called, "Hey, Mr. Snarly. Are you going to try a Tomb Room?"

A mischievous grin came over Mr. Snarly's face as he called back. "You'll see."

Sneak Peek!
From *Chaos at Camp Clover* Book 4

"We got this! Twenty yards to go, mateys!" Owen held up his paddle in the direction of the finish line.

Dozens of kids on shore were jumping up and down cheering the racers on.

"Too bad Jason isn't here," Stanley said. "He's wanted to win the row boat race ever since we started coming to Camp Clover."

"I hope he's better soon," said Owen.

Beth was breathing hard in between strokes, but managed to get the words out. "We should give him the trophy."

Owen and Stanley nodded their heads in agreement.

"Ten yards!" shouted Owen.

Stanley glanced back to check out the boats behind them. "No one's even close!"

For a moment, Beth held her paddle still and closed her eyes. She pictured them giving the trophy to her cousin. He'll be so psyched that the Mayville Campers are finally row boat champions.

Beth's eyes popped open. Her toe felt funny. No—her whole foot felt weird. She looked down to see her sneaker submerged in water. "Uh—

guys. We've got a problem."

Stanley and Owen's mouth's dropped open as they followed Beth's gaze to the bottom of the boat.

"What? Where's the leak?" Owen said lifting his feet.

As Beth and Owen desperately searched for the hole, Stanley cupped his hands and began scooping water from the boat.

Owen gave Stanley a dirty look as he frantically started scooping water himself. "I told you not to have that third piece of pie last night."

"Don't blame this on me," Stanley yelled.

"Stop it you two! Just keep bailing," Beth said.

The water rose below their seats. The rim of the boat was inches from the top of the water.

"So much for being champions this year," Stanley moaned.

"Wait! Look!" Beth was pointing to the boats behind them. In every boat kids were desperately scooping water just like them. "It's not just us. It's happening to everyone!"

Stanley slowly stood up and tried to balance.

"What are you doing?" Owen shouted.

Stanley took an awkward leap and did a belly flop into the lake. His head popped out of the water. "It's every camper for himself." He started swimming toward the shore.

"Come on, Beth!" Owen tightened the strap on his life vest and dove into the water.

Beth took another look behind them. Other campers were jumping into the water as each rowboat slowly tipped and sunk below the lake's surface.

Beth dove in and began paddling backward as she watched the chaos in the water. "He's back," she murmured to herself. "Hector McGreevy, destroyer of all things fun, is back to start trouble at Camp Clover."

Beth turned toward shore and began swimming as hard as she could. "I have to tell Jason."

Kid's Page ~ Jason's Coin Rolling Trick

In Chapter 10, Jason is trying to roll a coin across his fingers.

The Coin Roll is an impressive trick to show your friends, but be warned—it takes a lot of practice and perseverance.

You must start super slowly and practice every day to have success.

You can get good at almost anything if you just practice a little each day.

It is all about teaching your muscles and your mind to perform the correct motions.

Practice does not make perfection, but it does make progress.

Check out these YouTube Tutorials to get started

"Coin Trick: How to Roll a Coin Across Your Knuckles" by S2Kards

"How to Roll a Coin Across Fingers" by December Boys

Good Luck!

Helping Your Child Make the Transition to Chapter Books
A Free Resource Guide for Parents

Hello Parents,

Is your child starting to read chapter books? If so, this is a time to promote independence while also ensuring that your child is reading for meaning.

To assist parents, I have created a helpful resource guide called,

Helping Your Child Make the Transition to Chapter Books.

The guide contains questions that will promote discussion and show you that your child is understanding the story even if you haven't been reading along. These generic questions are suitable for most any fiction book.

To get your free copy,

go to **pamelatraynor.com**

The *Parent Resource Guide* can be found on the Freebies tab.

When you join my mailing list, you and your child will also be notified of new book releases.

I hope your child is enjoying the Glowing Mystery Series and that you find the *Resource Guide for Parents* helpful.

If you could please take a moment to give a review on Amazon, it would be so helpful to me. A review is like a cheer, a high five and a hug all rolled into one.

Thank you, Pamela Traynor

Pamela Traynor writes books for children of all ages. Her picture book, *Grandparents' Day* won a 2018 Best Book Award. *Fiasco at the Fair*, the first book in the Glowing Mystery Series, received the Reader's Favorite 5 Star Review. Pamela is an elementary school teacher. She lives in New York with her family.

Maaz Farzaan is a self-taught artist and nature lover from India. He has been drawing since he was a child. Maaz enjoys illustrating books for children.

Made in the USA
Middletown, DE
22 February 2020

85192338R00073